W9-BZB-060

16

The Harmonica

Tony Johnston

Illustrated by Ron Mazellan

ᴎᴎ Charlesbridge

I cannot remember
my father's face,
or my mother's,
but I remember their love,
warm and enfolding
as a song.

Singing was like breathing
to us. For a time
the only music in our house
was our own voices—my father's, my mother's,
and mine—so off-key
we could crack crockery.

Then the melodies of Schubert
soared into our home,
freed from the neighbors' gramophone.

We sang and we listened
to the gramophone's sweet notes,
and we lived our lives. I had dreams
of music.

A piano was my heart's desire.
A piano for playing Schubert.
But like the composer, we were poor
as pigeons.
Even so, one evening, dusted
with coal from the mine
where he worked,
my father came home
and slipped a silvery gift
into my hand.
A harmonica.

On it were his charry
fingerprints.

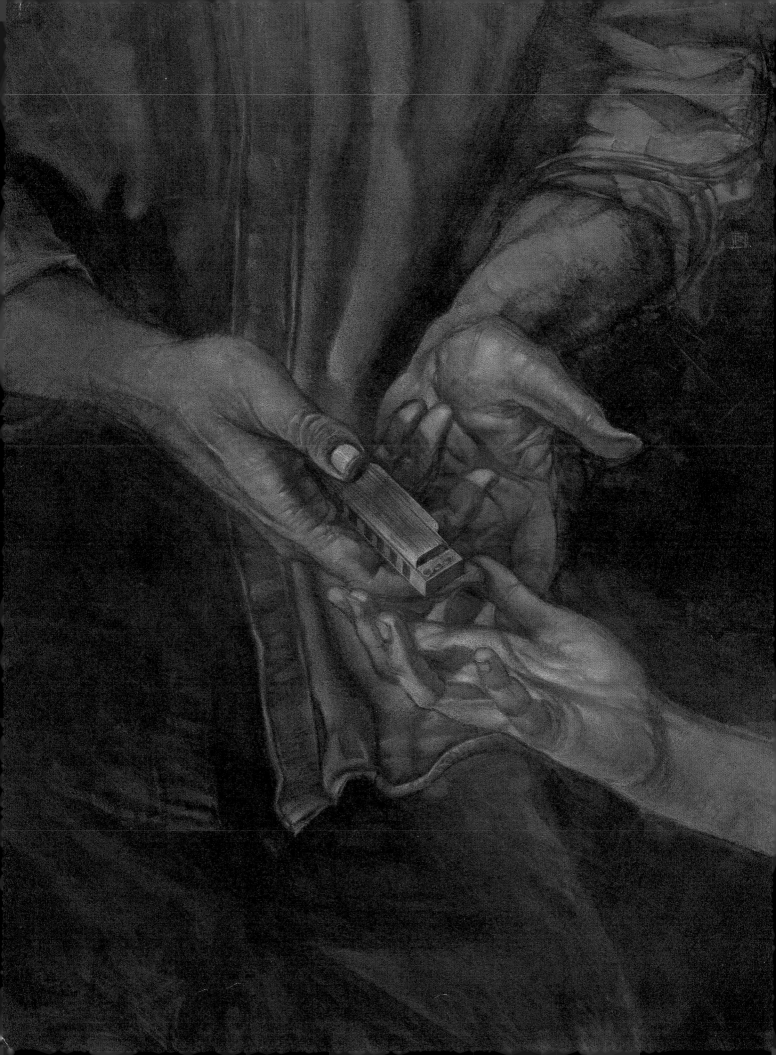

My lips loved the harmonica,
cool as water. At first my breath
panted in and out of its niched
sides like a bellows,
I was so eager.

"Gently," said my father, a smile
in his voice.
"Or you will simply blast it apart."

I wheezed. And blew. Until somewhere
in the heart of the harmonica,
my mouth found
Schubert.
Then my mother and father danced
together. Waltzed
over our bare floor.

Somewhere outside, a war
was raging. But it was far away—
a bad dream—leaving us untouched.

I played the harmonica
while my parents danced.
In our dream we believed
the world to be good. Until there
in the heart of Poland,
Nazi soldiers found us.

We were Jews.
Enough for them to take my mother
and father from me. Like a length of kindling,
in one stroke, they split
our family.

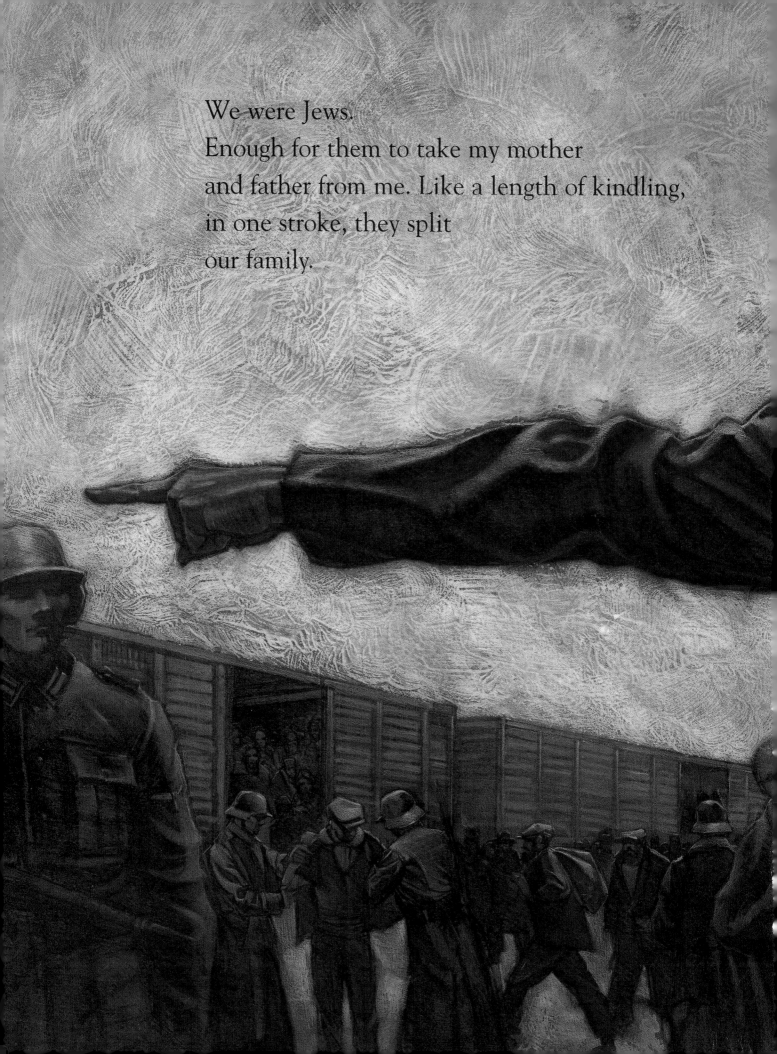

I was sent
to a concentration camp, swallowed,
dreams and all, down the dark
Nazi throat.
Barefoot, I labored alongside others,
all of us dull-eyed bags
of bones, digging a road through snow.

With each shovelful of frozen
earth, I thought of my mother and father.
Were they still alive? I wondered.

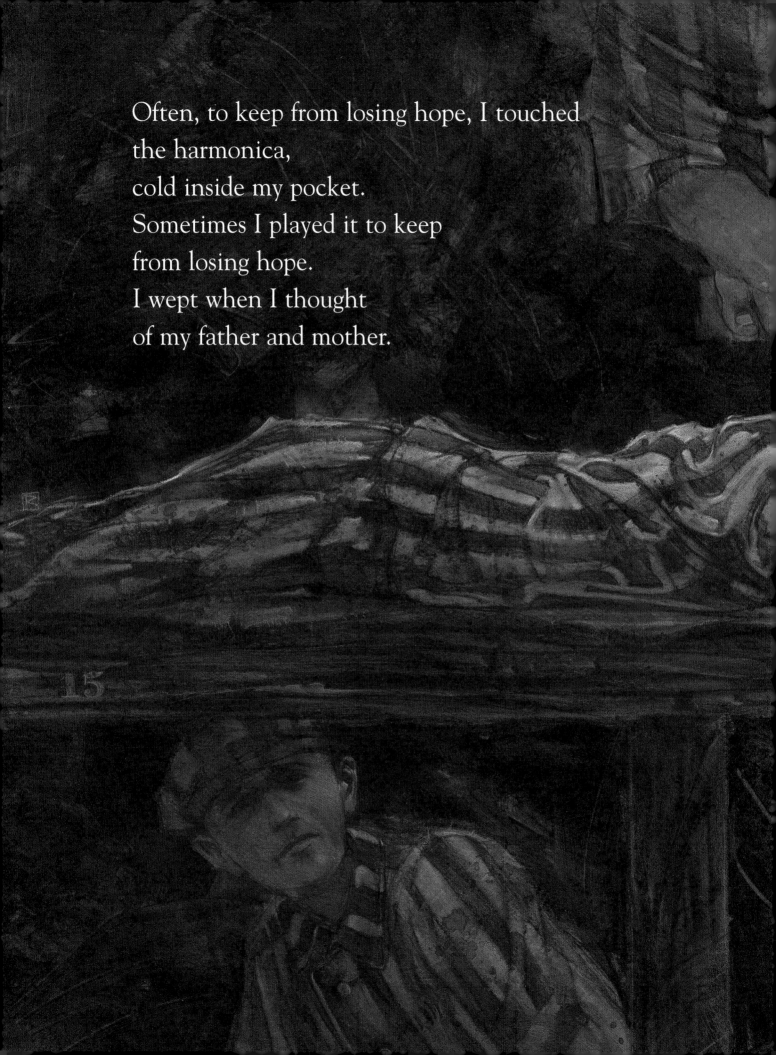

Often, to keep from losing hope, I touched
the harmonica,
cold inside my pocket.
Sometimes I played it to keep
from losing hope.
I wept when I thought
of my father and mother.

I awoke
jolted from sleep. And I knew—
my parents were dead.
Then I played Schubert.
Played and played while my heart
reeled.

The commandant of the camp loved
Schubert. By some terrible miracle
he heard of me
and sniffed me out.
One night he spat,
"Play, Jew!"

I stood before him, my hands numb
with winter. What if
I fumbled? What if
I ran out of breath? What if
the notes rushed from
my head?
Inside I trembled
like a hare crouched
in a bush. I had no doubt,
if I faltered, I would be
dead.

I remembered what my father had told me
of Schubert.
How he had lived in a bare room
with no fire. Though his fingers ached
with cold, he wrote his music.
Though he ached,
he could not stop creating
beauty.

Though I ached,
each night I, skin-and-bone-boy, played
for the commandant.
He listened, enthralled.
Each night, when I was done, he tossed
me bread.

He worked us, beat us for no reason,
without mercy. Yet
he recognized beauty. I could not imagine
how that could be.

I felt sick, black
inside, playing music
for the commandant, who wore
ugliness and death upon his shoulders
like epaulets.
I felt sick, getting bread
while others starved
to death.

I despised myself for every note,
every harmonica-breath until
one day a whisper grazed
my ear. "Bless you."
"For what?" I asked the dark.
"Schubert."

I slipped that into my pocket.
Each night, like the very stars,
my notes had reached
other prisoners.

"Play, Jew!"
The commandant spat, night after night.

Night after night
I touched the harmonica
to my lips. I thought of my father, who had given
it to me. Of my mother, who once
had danced. And of prisoners, without hope,
who might hear the notes
and be lifted, like flights
of birds.

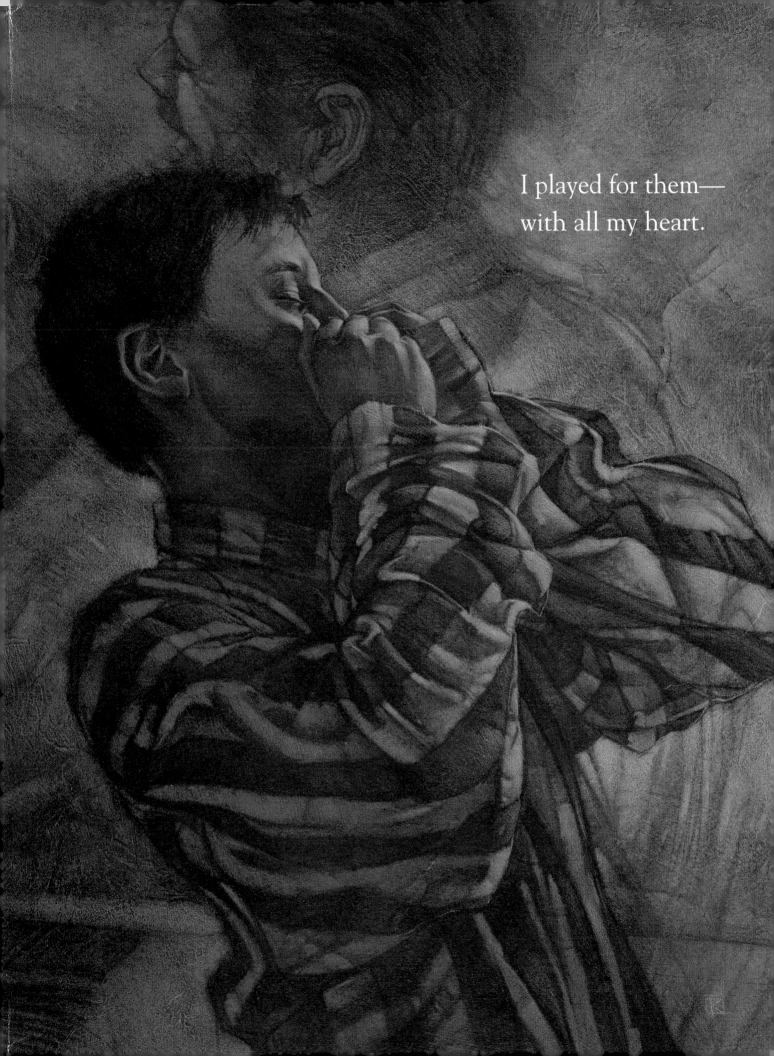

I played for them—
with all my heart.

THE HARMONICA was inspired by a true story. Henryk
Rosmaryn grew up in Czeladz, Poland. In 1939 the
Germans invaded his homeland. Henryk was taken to
Dyhernfurth concentration camp where, with the help
of the harmonica that his father had taught him to play, he
survived the hardship and sorrow of that prison.

   After the war he came to the United States and changed
his name to Henry Rosmarin. Again with the aid of his
harmonica, he shared his wartime experiences with others,
especially teenagers, in the hope that they might bring
about a better future. Although he died in 2001, his is
an ongoing story of the power of music and the strength
of the human heart.

Published by Charlesbridge
85 Main Street
Watertown, MA 02472
(617) 926-0329
www.charlesbridge.com

Library of Congress Cataloging-in-Publication Data

Johnston, Tony.
   The harmonica / Tony Johnston ; illustrated by Ron Mazellan.
      p. cm.
Summary: Torn from his home and parents in Poland during World War II, a young Jewish
boy starving in a concentration camp finds hope in playing Schubert on his harmonica, even
when the commandant orders him to play.
   ISBN 1-57091-547-4 (reinforced for library use)
[1. Harmonica—Fiction. 2. Jews—Fiction. 3. Concentration camps—Fiction. 4. World War,
1939-1945—Fiction. 5. Holocaust, Jewish (1939-1945)—Fiction.] 1. Mazellan, Ron, ill.
II. Title.
PZ7.J6478Har 2004
   [Fic]—dc21   2003003730

Printed in Singapore
(he) 10 9 8 7 6 5 4 3 2 1

Illustrations done in mixed media on illustration board
Display type set in Ancient Script and text type set in Goudy
Color separations by Bright Arts (H. K.), Ltd.
Printed and bound by Imago
Production supervision by Linda Jackson and Brian G. Walker
Designed by Susan Mallory Sherman

JUV
EASY
Johnst- Johnston, Tony
on
            The harmonica

DUE DATE